ARTHUR'S VALENTINE

by
Marc Brown

LITTLE, BROWN AND COMPANY
New York   Boston

For Melanie, Lyn,
and Felice —
all of whom
I regard with
wonder and delight

Little, Brown and Company

Hachette Book Group
237 Park Avenue, New York, NY 10017
Visit our website at www.lb-kids.com

First Paperback Edition: January 1988

Little, Brown and Company is a division of Hachette Book Group, Inc.
The Little, Brown name and logo are trademarks of Hachette Book Group, Inc.

Library of Congress Cataloging-in-Publication Data
Brown, Marc Tolon.
   Arthur's valentine.

Arthur® is a registered trademark of Marc Brown.

   Summary: Arthur's wrong guess about the identity of the secret
admirer sending him valentine messages leads to teasing by the other
children, but clues in additional messages allow him to get his due.
   [1. St. Valentine's Day — Fiction. 2. Animals — Fiction] I. Title.
PZ7.B81618As   [E]   80-14001
ISBN 978-0-316-11062-4 (hc)
ISBN 978-0-316-11187-4 (pbk)

HC: 20 19 18 17
PB: 30 29 28

SC

Manufactured in China

Someone was sending Arthur valentines, and Valentine's Day wasn't until Friday. They were all signed "Your Secret Admirer."

Dear Arthur,
You
Tom
for
Y

I love
You smAck!
lips
your secret admirer

Your se

It was a real mystery.
Who was Arthur's secret admirer?
It might be Fern.

It could be Buster playing a joke.

Or maybe even Francine. She was
always teasing Arthur.

Arthur hoped it was the new girl, Sue Ellen.

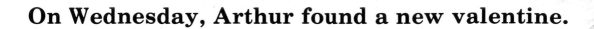

On Wednesday, Arthur found a new valentine.

Apples, Bananas, Peaches, a Pear,
With a face like yours,
You're lucky I care.
      Your Secret Admirer
P.S. In your lunch box you'll find a treat.
      It's just for you and it's extra sweet.

Arthur hoped it might be chocolate,
but at lunch he found this note:

> *Candy is sweet,*
> *Lemons are sour.*
> *I'll be watching you*
> *The whole lunch hour.*

Arthur looked at Sue Ellen.
She smiled.

Thursday, everyone made valentine boxes.
Arthur decided to make a special card instead.

When everyone mailed their valentines,
Arthur put his card in Sue Ellen's box.

Then, when nobody was looking,
Arthur hid the valentines
from the secret admirer
in his coat pocket.

After school, Arthur took off his coat
to play soccer and
all the valentines fell out.
Everyone laughed.
Buster called him "Loverboy."
"Hey, Hot Lips," shouted Francine.
Arthur left when everyone sang,

Arthur and his girl friend sitting in a tree,
K-I-S-S-I-N-G.
First comes love, then comes marriage,
Then comes Arthur with the baby carriage.

The next morning Arthur said he was sick.
"You don't want to miss
the big Valentine's Day party,
do you?" asked his mother.

Arthur went to school.
"Ick! Who sent this mushy valentine?"
said Sue Ellen.

"It's signed 'Arthur,'" shouted Buster.
Everybody laughed.
"Arthur loves Sue Ellen," everyone sang.

After school, Arthur wanted to be alone.
On the way home, he climbed up
to his tree house.
There he found another valentine.

I love you in London,
I love you in Rome.
Look in your mailbox
When you get home.
XOXOXOXOXOXOXOXOXOX
       Your Secret Admirer

"Oh, gross," said Arthur,
and ran into the house.

"I believe this is for you, Arthur,"
said his mother.
"It's a love letter," said his sister.

Arthur went to his room.
There was a movie ticket in the card.

My love, tomorrow is the day
We meet in row 3—
You in seat A,
Me in seat B.
          Your Secret Admirer

On the card, Arthur saw a smudge.
He looked very closely.
Something had been erased.
There was an F and an R and an A—
F-R-A-N-C-I-N-E!

The next day Arthur had a plan.
He ran to the movies so he wouldn't be late.

He found row 3.
He sat in seat A.

Francine smiled at Arthur.
"So you're the secret admirer," said Arthur.
"Good guess, Four Eyes!"

"Close your eyes," said Arthur. "I want to give you a kiss."
"Really?" said Francine.
"Close your eyes and count to ten."
"Okay," said Francine.

"Arthur, can I open my eyes yet?" asked Francine.